And We Will Be No More

by

Anne Schraff

Perfection Learning® Corporation
Logan, Iowa 51546-0500

Editor: Pegi Bevins
Cover Illustration: Doug Knutson
Cover Design: Deborah Lea Bell
Michael A. Aspengren

For information, contact
Perfection Learning® Corporation
1000 North Second Avenue, P.O. Box 500
Logan, Iowa 51546-0500.
Tel: 1-800-831-4190 • Fax: 1-712-644-2392
Paperback ISBN 0-7891-5247-9
Cover Craft® ISBN 0-7807-9649-7
Printed in the U.S.A.

1 When the baby girl was born in 1786, Deer Path, her mother, thought that her new daughter was very beautiful. Her smooth skin was the russet color of oak leaves on a fall day. And her dark eyes were bright and alert. When Loud Thunder saw his daughter, he said in a quiet, awestruck voice, "She is as dawn's light, like a shining." And so the girl was named Dawn Light.

Dawn Light was now 15. She lived with her family in a bark-covered longhouse in an Iroquois village. The village was located on the coastline of what is now the state of New York. Like all the girls of the turtle clan, Dawn Light helped her mother with an endless round of chores: cooking, cleaning, planting, and harvesting. But this morning the girl was having a hard time concentrating on her work. She was thinking about something that had happened the day before.

A runner had come into the village with news of a cabin being built on the other side of the forest. He said it belonged to a white-faced man and his family. Many

members of the tribe gathered around to
hear the runner's news.

"The man who raised the cabin has a
great red beard and a loud, booming
voice," said the runner.

"A red beard?" Deer Path asked. "It
must appear that flames are coming from
his face. Was he an angry and frightening
man?"

"Or perhaps a demon?" Loud Thunder
suggested.

"No," the runner assured them. "He was
quite kind to me. He and his family had
wonderful possessions. Great black
kettles, wondrous beads and jewelry,
colored cloth, and fine, sharp knives and
tools. He said he would soon come to our
village to trade if we would allow it."

Dawn Light trembled with excitement
as she tried to imagine the treasures. She
was especially interested in the beads and
jewelry. The beads the Iroquois made
were rounded out from shells or the teeth
of animals. What were the white man's
beads like? she wondered. She had seen
women of the bear clan wearing silver
necklaces they had gotten from the white

traders. Dawn Light had often dreamed of a silver necklace of her own and wondered if the red-beard had any.

"The less we have to do with whitefaces the better," Deer Path said quietly but firmly.

Dawn Light heard the warning in her mother's voice. The girl knew that white people had strange ideas that the Iroquois could not understand. Whitefaces believed that each person who raised a cabin owned the land around the cabin. They owned all the grass that grew on the land too.

The Iroquois questioned such a belief. How can one person own the grass all people walk on, any more than a person can own the air others breathe? they asked. Everyone knew that Ha-wen-ne-yu, the Good Brother creator, had made the air, the sky, the land, and the grass for all people to use.

"The red-beard wants beaver pelts," the runner said. "And we might have some of his kettles and knives if we trade with him."

He-Who-Dreams spoke up then. "I think to trade with the red-beard would be a good thing. I have seen the things the white people have, and we could make good use of them."

He-Who-Dreams was a *sachem*. *Sachems* represented the turtle clan at council meetings of the tribes in the area.

Dear Path was one of the mothers of the turtle clan. Dawn Light's grandmother, Cloud Shadow, was the head mother in the clan. Cloud Shadow had great power. She made the final decision in important matters. The mothers chose the *sachems*, who voted in the councils.

Now Deer Path said, "If we trade with the red-beard, more whitefaces will come looking for our beaver pelts. And they will build cabins. Then they will want the land we love and the streams that give us life."

Dawn Light saw the logic in her mother's reasoning. But she was eager to see the red-beard's goods. She was glad when some of the women spoke up.

"I would like a kettle that does not crack," one of the women said.

"And I would like some brightly colored cloth," another added.

Cloud Shadow looked around at the group of women. She was a wise leader, and she always listened to what others had to say. Now she said, "Perhaps we should make friends with some of the whitefaces and trade with them. Then we will have allies if other white people come to harm us."

Many in the group nodded at the wisdom of Cloud Shadow's words.

"If the red-beard is truly a good man," the old woman continued, "then I think we should trade with him."

There was a murmur of assent from the other women. All except Deer Path, who did not think having anything to do with white people was a good idea. But the decision was made. The red-beard would be invited to show his wares in the village and to examine the beaver pelts the Iroquois had.

As they returned to their chores, Dawn Light thought about the whitefaces. Did they really have canoes as big as longhouses as some of the elders of the tribe said? she wondered. And what was it like across the great sea from where they had come? Was it better there? It must not be, or why would they have come here?

Later, Dawn Light asked her father about the whitefaces. Over the years, he had met many of them and had even learned to speak English fairly well. "Father, what are the whitefaces like?" Dawn Light asked.

Loud Thunder smiled at his daughter in his gentle way. "As with all people, some are good, and some are bad," he replied. "Two Iroquois from the beaver clan once walked across the grass where a white man had built his cabin. The white man shot them both. He said it was a crime to walk on another man's grass. The white man's court agreed and said the man had done no wrong in shooting the Iroquois."

"We know that the red-beard is friendly. Perhaps he is honest as well," Dawn Light said hopefully.

Her mother turned from the fire, her face scornful. "Do not imagine goodness unless there is proof of it," she advised. "Do you invite a rattlesnake into your longhouse just because he is not shaking his rattles?"

Dawn Light could see that talk of the white man upset her mother. So she said no more.

When darkness came, Dawn Light crawled onto a platform in the longhouse. There she slept on a beaver-pelt robe. The early spring nights were still cold. But the robe was so soft and warm that she was usually able to fall into a restful sleep. As she did every night, she silently thanked the beaver for his warm fur. Then she closed her eyes and waited for sleep. But tonight the light of the moon shone through a crack in the wall and made her restless.

It would not be long before Dawn Light would be married. Already her mother was talking to the mothers of some of the young men in the village. Deer Path had promised the girl that she would not choose a husband that Dawn Light truly hated. But Dawn Light's problem was that she had yet to find a boy in the village that she even *liked*.

Her mother scoffed at such thoughts. Deer Path said that marriage had nothing to do with feelings. Marriage was like a business arrangement. And the elders knew who was suitable for whom. It had always been like that, Deer Path said, and so it would always be.

Now Dawn Light tossed and turned on her beaver robe, wondering what it would be like to be married. She supposed she would do the same chores she was now doing, only she would have a husband. And soon she would have children. Dawn Light wondered about the white-faced people from across the sea. Was this how they lived too? Did the elders of their tribes arrange marriages for them?

"Go to sleep, sister," Dawn Light's older brother, Black Wing, complained. "You are making the platform groan with your tossing."

"I am sorry, Black Wing," Dawn Light apologized. As she struggled to lie still, she thought of Falling Water, a boy from the village who was of the age to be married. Deer Path and Falling Water's mother had spoken about a possible marriage between their children. But Dawn Light did not like the idea. Falling Water was a tall, handsome youth, it was true. But Dawn Light thought he was too wild and haughty. She wanted a boy like her own father, gentle and full of quiet strength.

"I don't want to marry Falling Water," Dawn Light whispered into the darkness of the longhouse. "I cannot. If I am forced to marry him, then I will divorce him at once. I will throw his possessions outside the longhouse and be done with him."

"Sister, you are troubling my sleep," Black Wing insisted. "You will marry the man the old ones tell you to marry. It is not for you to decide."

"But he is arrogant, brother," Dawn Light complained. "He acts as if he's the most important person in the village. How can I marry someone like that?"

"Go to sleep, little sister!" Black Wing implored.

Dawn Light sighed. Would she be forced to marry Falling Water? she wondered. And if not him, then who would it be? In her mind, she began recalling the boys of the village one by one. But before she could finish, she succumbed to the warmth and softness of the beaver-pelt robe and drifted off to sleep.

* * *

Two days later, Gray Shell appeared at Dawn Light's door. Gray Shell was Dawn Light's cousin and closest friend. "Hurry!" Gray Shell cried. "Two whitefaces are here to trade!"

Dawn Light dropped the basket she was working on and hurried away with her cousin. They joined the group of villagers that had gathered around the traders.

One of the traders was a huge man with a red beard sprouting from his face. He had merry blue eyes, and he smiled cheerfully. Dawn Light decided that he was the red-beard the runner had told them about. The other was a boy about 16 years old. The boy had yellow hair and eyes the color of robins' eggs. Dawn Light found that she could not take her gaze from those piercing, light-colored eyes.

The two girls stood with the others while the white men laid out their goods.

Dawn Light craned her neck to see if they had silver necklaces among their wares, but she didn't see any.

Loud Thunder spoke in English with the two traders. He told the tribe that the older man's name was Mort Cairns and the younger man was his son Jeremy.

By the time the trade was made, Mort and Jeremy Cairns had a basket full of corn seed and a stack of beaver pelts. In exchange, the villagers received two large black kettles, four knives, two bolts of colored cloth, and some beads.

As the onlookers returned to their longhouses, Mort Cairns began to speak with Dawn Light's father. The two men talked of hunting.

"Your men should use traps, Loud Thunder," advised the white man.

Loud Thunder shook his head and said in English, "My bow and arrow cause brother beaver no suffering. The kill is quick and clean. Traps are cruel and painful. It is not right to use them."

"But you would get many more beaver using traps," Mort Cairns countered.

"Brother beaver gives us his gift of

warm fur. Why bring him suffering?" Loud Thunder asked.

Cairns laughed and said, "I know of no beavers I'd call brother. I just see them as a way to make a living."

Jeremy Cairns spoke up then. "Loud Thunder is right, Pa. It would be better to kill the beaver quickly and painlessly."

"What did the yellow-haired boy say, Father?" Dawn Light asked quietly.

Loud Thunder translated for her. Dawn Light was touched by the boy's words. She had hardly taken her eyes off him. She marveled at his nice, smooth face and shiny, golden hair. She wished he were an Iroquois of marriageable age. She decided that if he had been born an Iroquois, his mother would have named him Golden Mane.

But all that was a dream, and Dawn Light knew she dreamed too much. She also knew she liked jewelry too much. But still she drew a little closer to her father and asked softly, "Do they ever have silver necklaces to trade?"

"Do you know of silver beads?" Loud Thunder asked. He did not know the

English word for "necklace." Dawn Light stared shyly down at her own moccasins.

Cairns didn't seem to understand Loud Thunder's request. "What's she wanting?" he asked, smiling.

"My daughter saw silver beads on the women of the bear clan," Loud Thunder explained. He drew a loop around his neck with fingers.

Jeremy looked at Dawn Light then as if he was noticing her for the first time. "You mean a silver necklace," he said. Then he smiled and added, "Next time I will bring one for the pretty maiden."

Father told Dawn Light what the boy had said. Without even looking up, Dawn Light turned and ran into the longhouse. Once inside, she realized that her cheeks were on fire and her heart was pounding like a drum.

2 Early one morning, the women went into the forest to gather sap from the maple trees. They spent long hours over open fires in the forest, stirring the boiling syrup so it wouldn't burn. They then poured it into wooden troughs and stirred still more until the syrup turned into maple sugar. The sugar was preserved in little birch bark trays, where it hardened. It would be used for a long time to flavor foods.

Dawn Light loved making maple sugar and often sneaked a lump of sugar when no one was looking. She thought maple sugar was surely the tastiest treat on earth. She wondered what the family of the red-beard ate for treats.

After the rest of the women had returned to the village, Dawn Light lingered in the woods to look for feathers. She and her mother were making her a new cape. And Dawn Light wanted to decorate it with the cheerful feathers of the blue jay.

She headed toward the stream that ran through the forest. Birds often stopped at the stream to drink, and she hoped to find a stray feather on the bank. Suddenly she spotted a blue jay feather lying in the reeds next to the stream. The color of the feather reminded her of Jeremy Cairns' eyes, and she smiled.

With her eyes on the bright spot of blue, she headed toward it. Her eyes were busy, and her mind was occupied by thoughts of Jeremy. So Dawn Light did not see the trap hidden in the reeds. She stepped right into the steel jaws of the trap. It sprang shut around her foot, and she fell screaming to the ground.

Desperately she tried to pry the jaws of the trap apart. But the springs were so strong that she couldn't free herself. Pain shot up her leg, and her foot began to swell. In despair, she realized that at least some of the bones in her foot were broken.

Terror mingled with her pain as Dawn Light wondered what would become of her. No one had seen her lag behind to look for feathers. Back in the village, they probably had not even missed her yet. Dawn Light often went alone to the fields to hoe weeds. Her mother probably thought she was there. And no doubt Dawn

Light's father thought she was in the longhouse helping her mother. Her family might not realize for hours that something had happened to her.

"Help!" Dawn Light cried. She looked around desperately for someone—anyone to help her. But the only movement she saw was a group of beavers building a dam a little way downstream. This was the beavers' path to and from the stream, she realized. And that was why the trap had been placed there.

Suddenly she heard footsteps moving toward her. Someone was coming! Maybe her brother, Black Wing, or her younger brother, Rain-On-Wind, had heard her cries and had come searching for her!

"Help me!" Dawn Light cried out again.

But it was not her brothers who parted the reeds and stared down at her. It was two white-faced children, a girl of about 12 and a boy of about 14.

"Look, Meg! An Indian!" the boy exclaimed.

The girl came closer. "Her foot's caught in a trap! Josh, can we pry it open with a stick or something?"

Dawn Light didn't know what the two children were saying. But she thought she heard concern in their voices.

She watched as the boy found a stout stick and knelt beside her. Carefully he inserted the stick between the steel jaws and pried the trap open. The girl moved Dawn Light's foot free.

"There you go," Meg said, smiling.

Dawn Light smiled back. She nodded her thanks to the children and then started to get to her feet. She wanted to return to the village as soon as possible. There a shaman from the medicine society would heal her leg. But when she put her weight on the injured foot, a terrible pain shot up her leg. She fell back to the ground in a faint.

In her dazed state, she could hear the children talking to each other. Suddenly she felt her shoulders being lifted off the ground and then her legs. Dawn Light realized that the two children were carrying her. She wanted to protest because she didn't know these children and had no idea where they might be taking her. Perhaps they would lock her up somewhere, she feared, and she would not be allowed to return to her family. But she did not have the strength to say anything and allowed herself to be carried through the woods.

They carried her for quite some time, stopping now and then to take a break. Finally they reached a clearing where a cabin stood.

"Pa!" the boy called out. "We've got an Indian here!"

When Dawn Light saw the cabin, she started to panic. What will happen to me now? she wondered. Will they lock me in that cabin? She struggled to get to her feet again.

Just then the cabin door opened, and Mort Cairns came out. "What do you have there?" he called out to the children.

"This Indian girl got her foot caught in a beaver trap. We got her out, but she's wounded pretty bad," Josh explained.

"Her foot's all swollen," Meg said. "Some of the bones must be broken."

"You did the right thing by bringing her here," their father said. "Let's get her inside."

The big man leaned over and scooped Dawn Light off the ground as if she weighed no more than a baby. The girl was so frightened that she almost forgot her pain. She was heartened to see that the man was Mort Cairns. But even he was not well-known to her. The trader smiled and had merry eyes, but she didn't really know his heart. Didn't her mother say he might not be trustworthy?

Cairns carried her into the cabin and laid her down on a cot. One of the children brought a rolled-up quilt so that she could elevate her injured foot.

The woman who lived in the cabin bathed Dawn Light's foot in cool water. Then she applied a poultice of herbs to reduce the swelling. It was not so different from what the shaman would have done, Dawn Light thought, and she was comforted.

The woman smiled at Dawn Light. She had fat yellow braids wrapped around her head, and her eyes were blue like Jeremy's. Despite her white skin and blue eyes, the woman had the same kind of motherly face that Deer Path had. A face full of compassion and concern. She brought Dawn Light a cup of hot tea.

As Dawn Light drank the warm, fragrant liquid, she took heart. She did not understand the language being spoken around her. But she had learned from her parents that by looking into the eyes of people, you could see their souls. And this family seemed to have good souls.

"She is the daughter of Loud Thunder," Cairns said. "I have seen her in the Iroquois village."

"Then we'd better take her home as soon as possible. They must be worried," the mother said.

"We'll take her tomorrow morning after she's had a chance to rest," her husband replied.

Jeremy entered the cabin then, fresh from fishing. He carried a fishing pole and a string of bass. When he saw Dawn Light, he hurried over to her.

"Are you all right?" he asked when he saw her injured foot.

Again Dawn Light did not understand the words he spoke, but they sounded kind. She nodded her head, not knowing what else to do.

Mort Cairns came over and spoke to his son then, and soon Jeremy left the cabin. A few minutes later, she heard a horse gallop away. Dawn Light hoped he was going to her village to tell her parents she was safe. She hoped she was right. Enough time had passed that she knew her parents would soon begin to worry about her absence.

Meg came over and sat on the edge of the bed where Dawn Light lay. She touched her chest and said, "Meg."

Dawn Light smiled back at her. The girl had a pretty, round face and red hair the color of her father's.

Meg once again touched her chest and said, "Meg."

Dawn Light realized she was telling her name. Dawn Light touched her own chest then and said in Iroquois, "Dawn Light."

Meg repeated it clumsily, and both girls laughed.

Later Meg brought Dawn Light a supper of rabbit stew and hot cornbread with maple syrup. The cornbread tasted so good and so familiar that Dawn Light had a second piece. So the people in the little log cabin liked maple syrup too! she thought.

After supper, the mother lit two oil lamps in the house. By the light of the lamps, Dawn Light could see the troubled face of Mort Cairns as he sat by the fire mending a chair leg. Maybe, Dawn Light thought, he had set the trap that she had stepped in. And if so, maybe he was afraid that the people of Dawn Light's village would no longer trade with him. Or perhaps he was afraid they would retaliate in some way.

Dawn Light and Meg spent the evening learning a few words of each other's language. Dawn Light quickly learned the words "cabin," "gun," "girl," "boy," and many others. In turn, Dawn Light taught Meg the same words in Iroquois.

That night, Dawn Light felt uneasy and did not sleep well. She was in the cabin of white people. Not on the beaver-pelt robe in her beloved longhouse with the familiar sounds of her family around her. Even though the Cairnses had been nice to her, bad dreams about white people filled her head. She dreamed of the whitefaces being as plentiful as ants in summer.

Sometimes Dawn Light had overheard her parents talking quietly at night when they thought the children were asleep. Now their conversations filled her dreams. "The whitefaces push us a little more every sundown," Deer Path would say. "They come to the forest and cut the trees. They build houses and put up fences. They claim that our people cannot go beyond the fences to gather acorns or take sap or pick berries. When I was a child, I saw perhaps four whitefaces in a year, and now they are all around us."

Dawn Light recalled in her dream the most frightening thing she had ever heard her mother say. "Someday the white-faced people will come to our village with guns," Deer Path had predicted. "They will drive us out into the wilderness and burn our longhouses. They will set fire to the treasures of our people, all the treaty belts and the wampum belts . . . everything dear to the turtle clan. And we will be no more . . ."

Those sad words echoed through Dawn Light's dreams. *And we will be no more . . . And we will be no more . . .*

Dawn Light awoke with a start. It would not happen. It *could* not happen! she told herself, her heart beating a wild tattoo. The village had stood for over two hundred years. The Creator had sent Deganawida, the great prophet, in a white stone canoe. Deganawida had taught the Iroquois tribes to get along with one another. And together they had formed the League of Five Nations. All the villages lived in harmony by the law of the League. It could not come to an end now . . .

Sleep did not return to Dawn Light for the rest of the night.

In the morning, after a breakfast of cornbread and tea, Dawn Light tried to stand on her foot again. But the pain was still too great for her to walk unaided.

Meg helped her out of the cabin where Jeremy was waiting with a horse. He smiled and hoisted her onto the horse's broad back. Dawn Light waved good-bye to the Cairnses then, and Jeremy led the horse into the forest.

Dawn Light had never ridden a horse through the forest before. It was fun to see the woods from a higher vantage point. The pathways through the trees were narrow, and sometimes Jeremy had to hold branches aside as the horse moved through.

When they reached the stream, Dawn Light pointed to where the trap that had caught her foot lay. Jeremy walked over and examined it. He pointed at his chest and shook his head.

"This is not our trap," he said.

Dawn Light did not understand his words, but she could tell by his gestures what he meant. She was relieved to find out that the Cairnses had not been responsible for what had happened to her.

When they finally reached the village, Dawn Light's heart was gladdened by the sight of her mother and father running toward her. As Jeremy lifted the girl down into her father's arms, other villagers gathered round.

"I am all right," Dawn Light told her father. "I stepped in a beaver trap."

"Yes, the boy came yesterday and told us," Loud Thunder said.

"We were worried, but he said his mother was taking care of you," Deer Path said. "We anxiously awaited your return today."

"Now more than ever I pity poor brother beaver to have such wicked things waiting for him in the brush," Dawn Light said. Many of the villagers nodded in agreement.

With a solemn look on his face, Loud Thunder turned to Jeremy. "Give our gratitude to your father and mother for their kindness to our daughter," he said.

"The trap that caught your daughter was not ours," Jeremy explained. "My father does not set traps where he knows your people walk. The trap must belong to another."

Loud Thunder translated for the group.

Dawn Light saw her mother's face darken, and she knew what Deer Path was thinking. If the trap did not belong to Mort Cairns, then it must belong to someone else. And that meant that there were still more whitefaces in the area.

"My father asked me to tell you that he wants to remain friends with your people," Jeremy went on. "We will make good trades as long as the seasons change. We will bring you fine tools and cooking utensils and cloth and beads." Then he looked at Dawn Light. "And a silver necklace for the pretty maiden."

Loud Thunder translated for Dawn Light. The girl blushed, but this time she did not run away. She told her parents how kind the Cairns family had been. And how they had cared for her in their little cabin as if she were their own child.

"My father also sent this warning," Jeremy said. "He says there are two brothers by the name of Casler in the area. They mean to trade beaver pelts with the Iroquois, but their goods are bad. Broken muskets and bad whiskey is what they're dealing. My father wanted you to know this in case they come to your village."

Again, Loud Thunder translated the boy's words.

"Thank you for the warning," Loud Thunder said. "We will watch for them.

Now, will you come into the village and take food and drink before you return to your cabin?"

"I'd like that," Jeremy said. Loud Thunder led the way with Dawn Light in his arms, and Jeremy and the others followed.

Dawn Light noticed that Deer Path walked slowly back to the village, a frown of deep concern on her face. But the other villagers, including her father, seemed pleased to entertain Jeremy Cairns. All that morning, there was a warm feeling between the villagers and the white-faced boy. It seemed as if the fears of both were needless. As if the villagers and the whitefaces at the other end of the forest could indeed live together in peace and prosperity.

3 A few weeks later, Dawn Light was helping her mother and grandmother prepare beaver pelts. Her foot had healed nicely, and she was back at chores. As they worked, several of the men and boys of the village gathered around a nearby fire to talk.

"We need more beaver pelts to trade," Dawn Light heard one of the men say. "We must range to the north."

"The Algonquin look for beaver to the north," Loud Thunder reminded him. "If our hunters come into contact with the Algonquin, there will surely be bloodshed."

Falling Water stood then and thrust out his chest. Dawn Light thought he looked like a silly rooster.

"Are we not brave warriors?" he demanded to know. "We will fight the Algonquin if they challenge us."

"You are young, Falling Water," Loud Thunder said patiently. "Some of the Algonquin have fine muskets. Ours are old and worn out. Even your great bravery cannot overcome the muskets they have."

"We too can get good muskets," Falling Water said. Dawn Light watched him with disgust. How arrogant he was, she thought again. She did not think him the least bit brave.

"Mort Cairns will not sell us guns," Loud Thunder pointed out.

"But I know of two white men who will sell us muskets," Falling Water boasted. "I know where their village is. I can go there and ask them to bring their muskets here to exchange for beaver pelts."

"Who are these men?" an old man asked.

"The brothers Casler," Falling Water replied.

"Mort Cairns claims they sell broken muskets," Loud Thunder said. "First they give the Iroquois whiskey to make them drunk, and then they trade broken muskets for fine beaver pelts."

"That is true," spoke up Cloud Shadow, Dawn Light's grandmother. "Mort Cairns says not to trade with such men."

"Of course he would say such a thing. He wants us to trade our beaver pelts to him alone," Falling Water said. "But why should we not make the best deal? Why should we not be armed well against the Algonquin if they threaten us?"

There was a loud murmur of agreement from the men. One old hunter said, "The Algonquin should not have better muskets than the Iroquois. If these Caslers will sell us useful muskets, then let us trade with them."

Black Wing spoke up then. "The Algonquin have no right to keep us from the forest to the north," he said. "If they challenge us, then we will fight them." Black Wing was just 16 and had yet to draw blood in battle.

Deer Path glared at her son and said, "If you bring warfare upon our heads, you will bring mourning to our longhouses."

"We will not bring mourning to the longhouses because we will defeat the Algonquin," Black Wing said. "I say we trade with the Casler brothers. We need new muskets."

His opinion was echoed then by most of the group.

"What do you think, Grandmother?" Black Wing asked. "Do you agree that we should trade with the Casler brothers?"

Cloud Shadow thought for a moment before answering. Then she said, "I think the men are right. We need to be armed in case we are attacked. We will invite the Casler brothers to our village to see what they have. If their muskets are good, we will trade with them."

"Good," said Black Wing, smiling.

Dawn Light looked at her brother. It made her sad to see how happy and excited he was at the thought of clashing with the Algonquin.

Later when they were alone, she reprimanded Black Wing. "Do you long to fight the Algonquin and die before you are old and gray?" she asked.

"I will not die, little sister," Black Wing laughed. "I will be a great hunter and a brave warrior. My enemies will fall like grass before the wind. I will bring glory to my longhouse and one day will become a Pine Tree in the village."

A Pine Tree was a person with force to his words. Someone the other members of the tribe listened to.

"Tell me, Dawn Light, who among the men of this village are the most honored, the most respected?" Black Wing went on. "The warriors, of course. If I wish to become a Pine Tree, I need only become a great warrior, and the honor is mine."

"But—" Dawn Light began. But her brother interrupted her.

"And how can I become a great warrior unless I fight?" he demanded to know. "But I cannot fight with a broken gun. Falling Water must bring the Casler brothers here, of that I am sure. So do not trouble your mind, little sister. What is right and necessary will be done."

* * *

The next week, the Casler brothers came to the village. Robert Casler was a tall, gaunt man whose hawk nose hung over a graying mustache. His brother Lewis was short and stout with a black beard. The two spoke the Iroquois language fluently and offered to trade two rifles for beaver pelts.

"We need more guns," He-Who-Dreams said. "Two is not enough."

"Sorry," Robert Casler replied, spitting

a stream of tobacco onto the ground. "Two's all we've got. We'll have more in a few days though."

Falling Water tried out both muskets. Each seemed to work fine. He smiled and nodded at Cloud Shadow.

"We will keep them," Cloud Shadow said. "Bring more later."

When the two brothers had left, Black Wing said to Loud Thunder, "Mort Cairns lies, Father. These are good muskets."

Loud Thunder shook his head. "I still don't trust the two brothers," he said. "Their mouths say one thing, but their eyes say another."

Despite Loud Thunder's objections, a hunting party of 15 warriors prepared to head north a few days later. Loud Thunder, Black Wing, and Falling Water were among them. Falling Water and another warrior would carry the muskets. The others were armed with bows and arrows.

Dawn Light watched as the group readied the horses. It bothered her to see the merriment in the eyes of the young men as they spoke tauntingly of meeting the Algonquin.

"The Algonquin call us wolves," Falling Water said.

"Then we will devour them!" Black Wing declared boldly.

All the young men laughed.

Dawn Light shook her head as the hunting party rode off. It was almost as if they hoped for a battle. She noticed that only Loud Thunder remained solemn as he left the village.

The next day, the Casler brothers returned to the village. Cloud Shadow, Deer Path, and many of the other women were in the woods gathering firewood.

"We have more guns to trade for beaver pelts!" the brothers called to the men who remained in the village. "And whiskey for all!"

They began passing the whiskey out to the men, who took it eagerly. Since the first trade with the Casler brothers had been good, they were open to more. But things did not go as well this time.

It sickened Dawn Light to see events unfold just as Mort Cairns had predicted. The whiskey dulled the minds of the Iroquois men, and they were soon too drunk to protect their own interests. By the time the Caslers were finished, they were two dozen beaver pelts richer. And the Iroquois men were left with several worthless muskets and a few dull tools.

As the Casler brothers left the village, Lewis Casler spotted Dawn Light carrying water to her longhouse. A smile crossed his face.

Dawn Light felt uneasy. On him a smile looks like it does on the face of a coyote, she thought. She could almost imagine him licking his chops as he gazed at her.

"Go ahead, Robert," Lewis Casler said. "I'll catch up with you."

He approached Dawn Light then. "What a pretty maiden you are," he said in Iroquois. "What is your name?"

Dawn Light looked into the man's eyes and discovered that his soul was dark. She turned away without answering him.

Lewis Casler dug into a leather pouch and withdrew a necklace of brilliant blue beads. He held it up, and the sunlight shone through the beads like blue fire.

"I've got beads," he said. "Pretty blue beads."

Dawn Light turned then and looked at the necklace. She gasped at its beauty. She had never seen beads of that color and longed to touch them. But she didn't say a word. She even pretended to be disinterested. She wanted nothing to do with the evil man who gave whiskey to the Iroquois in order to cheat them.

Casler shrewdly noticed that the girl had been drawn to the beads. Calmly he walked over to where the village met the forest and dropped the necklace at the base of an oak tree. Dawn Light's eyes widened at the man's actions. Then Casler smiled at her and walked out of the village.

Dawn Light was confused. Was he leaving the blue beads behind in the hopes that she might like him? she wondered. Or was he throwing away the beads because she had insulted him by not speaking to him?

Dawn Light went back to work then and tried to forget about the necklace. But from time to time, she found herself stopping in front of the longhouse, gazing at the oak tree.

Were the beads still there? she wondered. Or had a villager come along and taken them? Or had the beads ever been there in the first place? Might Casler have only pretended to cast the beads away? Perhaps he had kept them in his hand the whole time and was now laughing at how gullible Dawn Light was.

It does not matter, she told herself. If the beads are there, I will not go near them. And if they are gone, so much the better.

But as the day wore on, she became more and more preoccupied with the thought of the necklace lying under the tree. Try as she might to forget about it, the beautiful blue color of the beads was stuck in her mind.

Finally at dark, she decided to have a look. It can't hurt, she told herself. If the beads are there, I'll simply look at them and then put them back.

Dawn Light walked slowly to the oak tree. She peered along the ground, looking for the necklace. Soon she saw the beads, shining like heavy drops of dew in the sparse light of the moon. She reached out and touched them gently to make sure they were solid and real. They were so smooth, her fingers almost slid off their surface.

Dawn Light sighed in awe and longing. They were the most beautiful beads she had ever seen. She reached down and picked them up, wondering how they would look on her.

Dawn Light raised the necklace over her head and let it slide down her hair and around her neck. Even though she could not see her reflection, she felt beautiful. She touched the beads again, stroking their smoothness and smiling. Then she stood up, wondering again why Lewis Casler had left the necklace behind. Should she keep them? She shook her head and scolded herself. She could not possibly keep something that had belonged to such an evil, dishonest man. But at the same time, the thought of leaving such a beautiful work of art lying on the ground was almost unbearable.

Suddenly Dawn Light heard a rustling noise, and Lewis Casler stepped out of the woods.

"I thought I might find you here," he said in Iroquois.

Immediately Dawn Light removed the necklace. "I'm—I'm sorry. I must go," she said. She started to lay the beads back under the tree, but Casler's next words stopped her.

"You know that the spirit of the beads now lives within you," he said.

Dawn Light looked doubtful.

"Well, isn't it true that the corn and the squash and the beans have spirits?" he asked.

Dawn Light nodded.

"Well, the beads have a spirit too," the man said. "Why do you think they shine as they do? That's the presence of the spirit within them. By wearing the necklace, you make a promise not to offend the spirit."

When Dawn Light still made no reply, Casler continued.

"It is a beautiful piece, isn't it?" he asked. "It was made for my grandmother in France. But I have given it to you, beautiful Iroquois maiden, because your grandmother is the head mother of your village. She can decide if your people are to continue dealing with my brother and me or with Mort Cairns. Speak to your grandmother on our behalf. And I will allow you to keep the beads."

Dawn Light wished she had never come here to recover the necklace from under the oak tree.

"Mind me, maiden. If Cloud Shadow convinces your people to continue to trade with us, then the spirit of the necklace will bring you and your village good fortune," Casler said. "If, however, you choose not to help us, then the beads will wreak vengeance on the entire turtle clan!"

4   Dawn Light hurried back to the longhouse, lifting the necklace off as she ran. She had made a terrible mistake! Her vanity had caused harm to herself and maybe to the whole turtle clan! Now there was dreadful magic in the blue beads.

As Dawn Light passed the stream, she paused. Would throwing the beads into the water take the bad spirits away? she wondered. She looked down at the necklace in the palm of her hand. How could something so beautiful possibly cause harm?

Maybe Lewis Casler was lying, she thought. Maybe there was no spirit in the beads. He was obviously a dishonest man, so why should she believe him? But, then again, how could she take the chance? Spirits were dangerous and easily angered. So what should she do? she wondered. If there was a spirit, throwing the beads away might anger it. But if she wore the beads, everyone would want to know where she got them. And what would she say?

No, she knew she could not wear the

necklace. But how could she protect herself and the village from the bad spirit in the beads? she wondered.

She decided that for now she would hide the beads under the beaver-pelt robe she slept on. Whenever she lay down on the soft fur, she had kindly thoughts of the beaver. Surely the good spirit of the beaver would overcome any bad spirit in the beads.

When she entered the longhouse, she saw that her mother and grandmother were working on deerskin dresses by the light of the fire.

"We never had to search for beaver and deer before the whitefaces came," Deer Path was saying. "Our needs were small, and there was plenty of beaver for all. Now we have greater needs. We want more and more pelts to trade with the white people for their goods. The whitefaces have infected us with the desire to have things we do not need."

Cloud Shadow shook her head. "Would you give up all that we have gotten from the white traders?" she asked. "Would you go back to the stone tools now that we have metal ones? Would you give up the Sheffield knives for sharp stones?"

"Yes, I would," Deer Path said sharply. "Our tools were fine until we saw the whitefaces'. Our bows and arrows were fine until the whitefaces brought us muskets. Now my son and husband range far north for beaver and may fall to an Algonquin musket."

Cloud Shadow frowned. She was much older than her daughter, but she was more willing to embrace new things. She liked the way the metal knives and the kettles made of iron and brass made their lives a little easier.

"Besides, the white man is not to be trusted," Deer Path went on. "Look what the Casler brothers have done. They gave us good muskets the first time to gain our trust. Then today, they got our men drunk, took more of our beaver pelts, and left us with worthless goods."

"That is true," Cloud Shadow admitted. "And we will not trade with those men again. But men like Mort Cairns *can* be trusted. Look what he and his family did for Dawn Light."

Dawn Light started at her grandmother's words. Cloud Shadow had decided not to trade with the Caslers again! What would happen now? Would the spirit of the necklace bring misfortune to her people? Or would an angry Lewis Casler come back looking for her?

Trembling inside, Dawn Light made her way to the other end of the longhouse as the women continued to talk.

"I still say the less we have to do with the whitefaces, the less we'll have to regret in the end," Deer Path said, standing firm in her opinion.

When Dawn Light reached her bed, she glanced at the two women. They were preoccupied with their sewing and their conversation. Quietly Dawn Light slipped the necklace under her beaver-pelt robe.

Just then her mother noticed where her daughter was. "Are you going to bed so soon?" Deer Path asked.

"Um, yes," Dawn Light replied. "I'm very tired tonight."

"All right. Good night, then," Deer Path said, returning her attention to her sewing.

Dawn Light lay down on the beaver-pelt robe. Through the soft fur, she could feel the necklace beneath her. It was as if the bad spirit in each bead was prodding her, punishing her for what she had done. She tried to think good thoughts about the beaver to quell the bad spirit. But tonight the good thoughts would not come. Over and over, the image of Lewis Casler's face drifted into her mind as a dark cloud drifts across a stormy sky. And all she could think about was the harm she might have brought to the village—or to herself.

* * *

The next morning, Gray Shell and Dawn Light went into the forest to search for mulberries. It was early summer now, and the forest was beginning to bestow its many gifts upon the Iroquois. As the girls walked along, Gray Shell chattered merrily. But Dawn Light was quiet. She was tired from lack of sleep and worried about the necklace.

Gray Shell noticed her cousin's silence.

"What's wrong, cousin?" she asked. "Is something troubling you?

"I'm fine," Dawn Light said, forcing herself to smile. "Just tired, that's all. I didn't sleep very well last night." She was ashamed of what she had done and had made up her mind not to tell anyone.

Gray Shell shrugged, and the two continued on. Soon they stopped at a mulberry tree, heavy with plump, purple berries. For a few minutes, the girls worked in silence.

Finally Gray Shell paused and turned to her cousin. "Dawn Light, I know something is wrong. Won't you tell me what's bothering you so that I can help you?"

Suddenly tears sprang to Dawn Light's eyes, and she found herself telling Gray Shell everything—about the necklace, about Lewis Casler's threat, about her grandmother's decision not to trade with the Caslers again. When she was finished, she hung her head. Telling someone what she had done had made her more ashamed than ever.

"You must not serve Lewis Casler's evil purposes," Gray Shell said.

"But, Gray Shell, I told you what Lewis Casler said. If I don't do his bidding, misfortune will strike me and maybe the whole turtle clan," Dawn Light said.

Gray Shell shook her head. "There is no spirit in the beads," she said.

"But how do I know that for sure?" Dawn Light asked. "There are spirits in corn and beans and squash."

"Those things are different," Gray Shell explained. "They come from the hands of the Creator. But the beads are from the hands of men—white men even."

"Why didn't I think of that?" Dawn Light asked. "Lewis Casler scared me so that I was not thinking logically. Of course there are no spirits in the necklace, for it was made with human hands. Oh, Gray Shell, I'm so glad I talked to you. I feel so much better now that I don't have to worry about harm coming to our village."

"You must cast the necklace into the stream," Gray Shell continued. "If the wicked man returns, tell him what you have done and that you are finished with him forever."

Dawn Light nodded. Gray Shell was

right. The sooner she was rid of the white man's necklace, the better.

When the girls had filled their baskets with berries, they returned to the village. The first thing Dawn Light did was retrieve the necklace from under the beaver-pelt robe. She put it in a small leather pouch. Then she hurried toward the stream with every intention of doing what Gray Shell had advised.

Dawn Light went to where the stream was widest and deepest. Then she pulled the beads from the pouch. But as she did, the sun caught the beads in its rays. And Dawn Light gasped as she was again struck by their beauty.

How could she throw such a beautiful necklace away? she asked herself. She sat at the water's edge, caressing the beads. After all, she thought, the beads have no bad spirit, so they are harmless. It would be a shame to lose them forever at the bottom of the stream. Perhaps she could simply hide them again in another place. No one but she would have to know about them. And she could take them out whenever she wished, just to admire their beauty.

She looked around then and spotted an unusual tree with twisted limbs not far from the stream. She went to the base of the tree and dug a hole. Then she buried the pouch with the necklace inside.

Now, Dawn Light said to herself, I can look at the beads when I want to. But they won't be in the longhouse to disturb my mind.

That night Dawn Light slept better, knowing that her village was safe.

A week later, the hunting party returned. The entire village turned out to welcome them home. There was much excitement when the villagers saw the numerous pelts the hunters brought with them. But the excitement vanished when they saw that an injured warrior lay across one of the horses.

"There was a short, fierce battle with a band of Algonquin hunters," Loud Thunder explained to the concerned villagers.

"Yes, four of them fell, but just one of ours," Black Wing boasted. "Falling Water shot one of the Algonquins, and his aim was true. But then another Algonquin shot him."

"The wound is not bad, but he has lost a lot of blood," Loud Thunder added.

Dawn Light gasped when she realized that the injured hunter was Falling Water. Her first thought was, "If he dies, I will not have to marry him." But immediately she felt ashamed of her selfishness. She should have thought of how heartbroken Falling Water's family would be if he died. Although she did not care much for Falling Water, he was a tall, handsome boy. And when the sun shone on his tall, coppery body he made a splendid sight. Surely his family treasured him.

Dawn Light watched the still form of the young man as he was carried into his longhouse. A shaman from the medicine society soon arrived.

The medicine man had a tiny embroidered pouch containing herbs, two cane whistles, a white weasel skin with more herbs wrapped in it, a horse chestnut, and dried eagle claw. He also carried a small wooden bowl, spoons, and eight tightly rolled pouches of herbs. The shaman went into the longhouse with Falling Water's parents.

Falling Water's other relatives followed—grandparents, aunt and uncles, brothers and sisters, and cousins. As Dawn Light watched them disappear through the door, she remembered the night she had spent in Mort Cairns' cabin. The Cairns family is so isolated, she thought. Just the parents and three children. When something bad happens, they have only each other to lean on for support. Here in the Iroquois village when trouble strikes, the entire relationship—and almost everyone else—turns out to support the family. Dawn Light could not imagine ever wanting to live isolated as the Cairnses did in that tiny cabin at the edge of the forest.

Dawn Light prayed as she and everyone else waited for word from Falling Water's relatives. "Oh, Creator, spare Falling Water because his mother and father and all his relatives love him," she whispered. "I am sorry for the wicked thought I had about him earlier. Please forgive me and allow only good to come to him."

The next morning, Falling Water's uncle came out of the longhouse beaming. Falling Water was a little better, he told the others. The boy had regained consciousness and was now sitting up drinking tea.

Everyone in the village celebrated. One of their finest young men would live. But no one was happier or more relieved than Dawn Light. Later that day, she asked Falling Water's mother if she might visit him.

"Of course," Little Tree answered. She looked pleased as she gave her permission. Dawn Light could tell that the woman hoped the visit would develop into something more.

Dawn Light entered the longhouse then. "I am glad you are better," she told Falling Water.

"Thank you," Falling Water replied.

Dawn Light could think of nothing else to say, so she added, "You are a warrior now."

She expected Falling Water to begin bragging about his new status, but instead he said, "Yes, I suppose I am. I have been wounded in battle, yet I still live."

To Dawn Light's surprise, the arrogance was gone from Falling Water's voice.

"The Algonquin warriors were brave," Falling Water continued. "I felt sad that I killed one of them. I thought of the sorrow that would be in his mother's heart when they took him home to her."

Dawn Light was amazed at the change in the young man. He had set out on the hunt with joy and enthusiasm, mocking the Algonquin and hoping for a confrontation. Now he spoke softly, almost humbly, about the battle. Dawn Light suddenly had new respect for the boy she had thought was foolish and shallow.

"I will bring you some fresh berries. They will make you stronger faster," she said.

"I will look forward to your return," Falling Water said.

As Dawn Light left the longhouse, she saw Black Wing and some of his friends gathered in a group nearby. They were laughing and mocking the Algonquin. Dawn Light noticed that her brother's voice was the loudest and most boastful of all.

It was obvious that the battle had given a measure of wisdom to Falling Water. But not to Black Wing.

5 "Tell me again," Gray Shell asked Dawn Light while they picked more of the quickly ripening berries in the forest. "What did the white man's cabin look like?"

"It was very small but sat in a large clearing," Dawn Light said. "Corn was growing on one square of land and other vegetables on another. Squash and tomatoes, I think. Besides their horse, they had a mule and a wagon. But such things would not be of much use in the forest."

"I have seen the big-wheeled wagons," Gray Shell said. "They look as if they would be fun to ride on. How far is the cabin from here?"

Dawn Light could see by the curiosity in Gray Shell's face that she wanted to see the cabin where the white people lived for herself. "If we run very fast, we could get there and back before sundown," she offered. "Would you like to do that, Gray Shell?"

"Oh, yes," Gray Shell said.

The girls put down their berry baskets and covered them tightly with bark. Then they sprinted through the forest until they reached the Cairnses' cabin.

"See?" Dawn Light whispered, even though they were still far enough from the cabin that no one in it could hear their voices. "They have cut all the trees in a big circle to make room for their crops and their animals."

"How many people did you say live in the cabin?" Gray Shell asked.

"Five," Dawn Light said. "It is very crowded inside. There are just two rooms. It is not like our longhouses where there are many rooms on either side."

"Where do the grandfather and grandmother and the rest of their relatives live?" Gray Shell asked.

Dawn Light shrugged. "I don't know," she said. "I think they must be far away, maybe on the other side of the great sea."

"I would miss my grandmother and grandfather very much," Gray Shell said.

"I would too," Dawn Light said. "I hope I always live in a longhouse with my whole family."

The sound of hammering suddenly

filled the air, and both girls turned their heads sharply.

"Where is that noise coming from?" Gray Shell asked.

"Over there," Dawn Light answered.

Silently, the girls walked through the forest until they came to a clearing. This one was brand new. The beginning of a log cabin was rising in the middle of the clearing. A woman was hanging out clothing to dry on a rope strung between two trees that had been left standing.

Dawn Light's eyes grew large with surprise. "More whitefaces!" she said. "Look, they are putting up a fence. This cabin is even closer to our village than the Cairnses' cabin."

Her surprise was soon replaced by fear. She knew that if more and more white people came, there would be no room for her people. There would be battles then between the white people and the Iroquois. And then the army would come with big guns, and the Iroquois would be doomed.

Dawn Light had heard what had happened in 1778 when she was ten. A big, white-faced general named John

Sullivan attacked Iroquois villages to the north, destroying their crops and orchards. Those Iroquois had fled the land. They went far north into Canada, leaving their burning longhouses behind them.

Luckily Dawn Light's people of the turtle clan were not bothered by General Sullivan. Her father had told her that the other Iroquois had made the mistake of siding with Great Britain in the big war. But the chief of the turtle clan made a treaty with the new government so that his people would not be driven out.

But still, in spite of the treaty, the white settlers kept coming, and nobody stopped them. Dawn Light knew that even if her people were not forced off their lands with guns, they would be driven away for lack of food.

The girls hurried back to the village then, picking up their berry baskets where they had left them.

"Mother!" Dawn Light called breathlessly as she ran into the longhouse. "There is a new cabin in the forest!"

Deer Path sighed and closed her eyes. "Is it closer to us than Mort Cairns' cabin?"

she asked. Dawn Light could hear the dread in her voice.

"Only a little closer," Dawn Light said.

Black Wing was sitting nearby restringing his bow. "Another place where we cannot hunt," he said in an irate voice. "More trees we cannot take sap from. Less room for the beaver and the deer. We need to stop them before they destroy the wilderness on which we live!"

The exhilaration from the first battle of his young life still coursed warmly through Black Wing's blood. It was obvious he felt as if he could triumph over any enemy.

"He-Who-Dreams will take this problem to the council," Deer Path said. "The council will talk to the white man's government and tell them our concerns."

"The government has ignored us before," Black Wing reminded her. "If the settlers continue to take our lands, I say we should deal with them as we dealt with the Algonquin hunting party!"

"Then the soldiers will come, my son," Deer Path said sadly. "As many soldiers as there are stars in the sky."

"Then we will fight the soldiers too,"

Black Wing declared. "What would you have us do? Wait until there is no forest left? Until we are starving, huddled under rags because there are no more beaver furs or buckskin from the deer? Must we wait until the whitefaces' fences surround us and we are dying? Better to die fighting than to die of starvation."

Black Wing's words scared Dawn Light. She didn't want fighting and bloodshed. But what if he was right? What if the whitefaces cut down the entire forest? The Iroquois would surely die.

She recalled her mother's sorrowful words. *Someday the white-faced people will come to our village with guns. They will drive us out into the wilderness and burn our longhouses. They will set fire to the treasures of our people, all the treaty belts and the wampum belts . . . everything dear to the turtle clan. And we will be no more . . .*

How could it be? Dawn Light remembered the kindly faces of the Cairns family, the mother with the yellow braids and the healing hands. Meg and Josh who had so kindly carried her from the forest when she was hurt. And handsome, blue-eyed Jeremy. They were friends, brothers of the Iroquois. Surely they did not intend to drive Dawn Light and her people from their village.

* * *

As the summer wore on, Dawn Light and Gray Shell often finished their chores quickly and then went into the forest to see if more whitefaces had appeared. Sometimes they hid in the thick woods and watched the finishing touches being put on the new cabin they had seen earlier.

One warm morning, right after the Green Corn Festival had ended, the girls saw a lot of excitement around the new cabin. The cabin was finally finished, and about two dozen white people had gathered to celebrate. Dawn Light could see Mort Cairns and his family among them, but she didn't recognize the others.

The air was filled with the savory aroma of roasted venison, and the adults stood around laughing and talking. The children ran back and forth, playing games and chasing each other.

Dawn Light worried about the number of white people she saw in the clearing. Did some of them plan on building cabins also?

Suddenly one of the children ran close to where Dawn Light and Gray Shell hid. The child's eyes widened as he spotted the two girls among the trees.

"Indians!" he yelled.

Everyone stared in shock toward the trees.

"Get inside the cabin!" one of the men shouted. Two men started shuffling the women and children into the cabin. Several others grabbed muskets and headed toward the girls.

Dawn Light grabbed Gray Shell's hand, and the two girls started running down the trail from which they had come. The girls ran fast, but the men chasing them had longer legs. Dawn Light stumbled on a tree root, and when Gray Shell was helping her to her feet, one of the settlers reached them. Then the others appeared. Two of the men seized the girls roughly, holding their arms behind their backs.

One of the men yelled something at the girls. When the girls didn't respond, he shoved them forward, indicating he wanted them to move.

Dawn Light and Gray Shell were marched into the clearing at gunpoint. Dawn Light expected the worst to happen. She thought they might be taken prisoner and would never see their families again. Or that they would be shot and killed! Every muscle in her body tensed with fear.

As they approached the cabin, she could see white faces peering at them through the windows. Suddenly she recognized one of the faces as that of Mort Cairns. Soon he was out the door and headed toward them.

"Likely these two girls are spying on us so their menfolk can come murder us when we least expect it," one of the men was saying to the others as Cairns approached.

"Don't hurt them!" he said. "I know these girls. I go to their village and trade with their people."

Jeremy, Meg, and Josh rushed to the sides of the two Iroquois girls. They

smiled at Dawn Light and greeted her as
an old friend. Jeremy surprised Dawn
Light by saying in hesitant Iroquois, "I am
glad to see you."

"I am glad to see you too," Dawn Light
replied. She wondered where he had
learned her language.

"You have nothing to fear from these
girls or from their people," Mort Cairns
told the men. "Let's allow them to be on
their way."

The men looked a little sheepish but
said nothing as they skulked off to eat.

As Dawn Light and Gray Shell turned to
leave, Jeremy said, "Soon I will have a gift
for you."

Dawn Light smiled. She already knew
what Jeremy's gift would be—the silver
necklace she had longed for. "I will have a
gift for you too," she said.

The girls waved good-bye then and
started down the trail into the forest.

"You see how kind Mort Cairns and his
family are?" Dawn Light said. "They cared
for me so tenderly when I caught my foot
in the trap."

"Some white-faced people are kind like

the red-beard," Gray Shell agreed. "But I think more are like the men who seized us. Those men see the Iroquois as wild animals that must be driven from the land so they can use it. We are in their way, and they will not stop for us."

"Mort Cairns and his family do not wish to drive us from the land," Dawn Light said firmly.

"Even the kind ones want us to stop being Iroquois and to become like them," Gray Shell said. "They want us to be like the Conestoga people who came to live among the white people."

"The Conestoga lived among the white people?" Dawn Light asked in disbelief. She had never heard of Indians living among white people.

"Yes, my mother told me," Gray Shell replied. "They lived in small houses, doing what the whitefaces did, farming the crops, cultivating their own little patches of land. But then one day a crime was committed, and the white people suspected a Conestoga man. Not long after, the white-faced men set the homes of the Conestoga on fire. When the

Conestoga came running out to escape the flames, the men killed them with muskets and hatchets."

"Even the children?" Dawn Light asked in horror.

"Yes," Gray Shell answered. "So you see, we would not be safe even if we gave up our beloved longhouses and lived among them."

Dawn Light did not want to believe Gray Shell. The forest was so large. Surely there was room for a few white people *and* the Iroquois village. If they traded with one another as friends as the Cairnses did, then why couldn't they share the forest?

As they made their way home, Dawn Light made up her mind not to think about Gray Shell's dire words. Instead she turned her thoughts to Jeremy Cairns, blue-eyed Jeremy with hair the color of corn. She pictured him coming to the village and giving her the silver necklace she had always dreamed of owning. She wondered what gift she might make for him.

These thoughts made Dawn Light

forget about the other necklace—the beautiful blue one hidden under the oddly shaped tree by the stream. And by now she had all but forgotten about the man who had given it to her.

6 Falling Water and Black Wing had become fast friends since the hunting trip. The bond between the two boys grew daily. And so did the shared resentment toward the encroaching white settlement.

A new family had built a cabin not far from the one Dawn Light and Gray Shell had watched being built. The family had three teenaged sons, and the boys had already raised Black Wing's anger. Black Wing had been stalking a deer one day with his bow and arrow. He was moving in for the kill when he was confronted by the boys. They menaced him with a musket and then tracked and killed the deer for themselves.

Black Wing and Falling Water spoke bitterly of the incident. "If I had carried a musket with me, I would have killed them!" Black Wing declared. "I may still do so!"

But Falling Water cautioned restraint. Dawn Light was encouraged to see him try to curb Black Wing's thirst for vengeance. Each day in small ways, Falling Water seemed to be growing in wisdom, she had noticed.

But one afternoon, Black Wing's anger over the stolen deer rose to a feverish pitch. Dawn Light overheard him complaining to Falling Water.

"The deer was mine," Black Wing insisted. "And the white-faced boys knew it. They are taking the food from our mouths, and I can no longer endure it. I will go to their cabin and steal the birds they keep in pens to pay us back for the deer."

"No, Black Wing," Falling Water said, placing a hand on his friend's arm. "You cannot do this. It will bring trouble upon the village."

"And isn't the stealing of our game bringing trouble upon the village?" Black Wing demanded. "Now we must do without the gifts the deer would have given us. Venison for many days, and deerskin for moccasins and dresses and breechcloths! Must I stand by and do nothing?"

Dawn Light turned to her brother. "Please don't do this, brother," she pleaded. "Don't bring trouble upon our village."

"Be silent, little sister," Black Wing said tersely. "No one will know what I have done. The white-faced man will blame a passing traveler who was hungry for roasted bird." Then he turned to Falling Water and said, "I am going tonight. Are you coming with me?"

Falling Water sighed. "Yes," he said, "I will come. If you've made up your mind to do this, perhaps I can at least keep you from being killed."

Dawn Light anguished over the boys after they left. She remembered the story her father had told her about the Iroquois who were killed for walking across a white man's grass. What would happen to Black Wing and Falling Water if they were caught stealing birds from the white man? she wondered. Surely they would be shot. And the whitefaces would probably lose no sleep over it. To them, it would be no more than shooting a raiding fox.

When the boys did not return to the village long after darkness had settled, Dawn Light was numb with fear. She waited outside the longhouse, telling her mother that she wanted to enjoy the warm night before going to bed.

Nervously she paced back and forth, peering down the dark path that led into the forest. Suddenly the moon surged through the clouds, and she saw Black Wing and Falling Water. They were in a merry mood. Each was carrying several dead chickens, their heads cut off and their feet tied with a buckskin thong.

"We have avenged the taking of the deer!" Black Wing cried jubilantly when he saw his sister.

"Yes, tomorrow we feast on fat birds," Falling Water laughed, holding up one of the birds for Dawn Light to see.

Dawn Light pulled Falling Water aside. "Why didn't you stop him?" she demanded. "How could you allow him to put himself—and our village—in such danger?"

"By the time we reached the whitefaces' cabin, Black Wing had decided that taking the birds was not enough. He wanted instead to challenge the oldest boy to a fight," Falling Water explained. "I talked him into settling for the birds. I thought it was less dangerous than the other plan."

Dawn Light was embarrassed by her outburst. She was grateful to Falling Water for what he had done. "Forgive me, Falling Water, for I spoke too quickly. Thank you for watching out for my brother's safety," she said.

Falling Water smiled. "He is my friend and like a brother to me. And you—"

Just then the door to the longhouse opened, and Deer Path and Cloud Shadow emerged.

"What is going on out here?" Deer Path asked.

Black Wing and Falling Water looked at each other. Then Black Wing said, "We bring fat birds to eat, Mother."

Deer Path peered at the birds in the moonlight. "Where did you get those birds?" she demanded. "They are not wild birds. They are the kind of birds the whitefaces keep behind fences. Where did you get them, my son?"

Deer Path's voice was stern. Dawn Light knew that if her mother found out that the boys had stolen from the white man—or anyone else—she would see that they were punished.

Black Wing hesitated and then said, "We exchanged the birds for a deer we had killed."

Cloud Shadow laughed scornfully. "You are fools then," she declared. "A deer is of much more value."

"Foolish boys," Deer Path said, joining in the ridicule. "When we pluck the feathers from the birds, we will roll you boys in grease and stick the feathers on your bodies—for all the village to see! They will all laugh when they are reminded of the ridiculous trade you made."

Deer Path watched Black Wing and Falling Water walk off in silence. They are afraid to admit what really happened, she thought. For if they do, they will be punished.

Everyone knew what the punishment for stealing was. First the thief was scratched with thorns. Then he was flogged with a leather thong. Dawn Light nodded knowingly as she watched Black Wing and Falling Water disappear into the village. Better to endure the ridicule of the women, she thought.

* * *

The next day, Mort Cairns and his children came to the Iroquois village. Dawn Light spotted them from her longhouse. She scooped up the basket of gifts she had prepared for them and ran outside.

Jeremy, Josh, and Meg turned and smiled when they saw Dawn Light.

"I have your gifts," Dawn Light said in Iroquois, pointing at her basket. She gave Meg a cornhusk doll that she and her mother had carefully crafted. Then she gave each of the boys a pair of moccasins. The moccasins were made from a single piece of buckskin, seamed over the heel and at the toe. Dawn Light had spent many hours decorating them with colorful beads.

Meg held up her doll and smiled. Dawn Light could tell she was very pleased with the gift. Josh pulled off his boots and put the moccasins on. "Look how fast I can run!" he shouted as he raced around the longhouse. Dawn Light did not understand his words, but she could tell that he, too, was pleased.

Jeremy laughed at his brother and then said in Iroquois, "These are fine moccasins, Dawn Light. Thank you."

"Where did you learn our language?" Dawn Light asked.

"My father has been teaching me," Jeremy answered. "He's learning it from the trading he does with the Iroquois."

He reached into his pocket then and brought out a leather pouch. "This is for you," he said, placing the pouch in Dawn Light's hand.

Dawn Light opened the pouch and looked inside. The silver necklace! She pulled it out and held it before her. It was even more beautiful than she had imagined it would be. The silver looked like water rushing over stones in a stream. She put the necklace on, and it lay around her neck, glistening and fluid on her russet-colored skin.

"Pretty maiden," Jeremy said.

He spoke in English, but Dawn Light remembered the words he had used the first time they had met. She smiled and felt a great rush of happiness.

She led the three children around the village then, showing them the longhouse and the fires and the orchard and gardens. When the Cairnses went home later that day, they took with them beaver pelts and left behind a copper kettle and some steel farm tools.

Dawn Light had a wonderful time with her three friends that day. And again the fear of the whitefaces pushing into the forest and driving her people away was abated.

* * *

Two days later Dawn Light was hoeing weeds from the rows of squash she had helped her mother plant earlier that spring. As she worked, she was thinking of Jeremy Cairns and smiling. "Pretty maiden," she said aloud in English.

"Pretty maiden!" she heard a deep voice echo. Startled, she stopped hoeing and looked up to see Lewis Casler watching her. Fear gripped her as she looked into his evil eyes.

"You did not keep your promise," Casler said. "Your menfolk just told me they had already traded their beaver pelts to Mort Cairns."

"I made no promise," Dawn Light said, squelching the terror she felt inside. She began hoeing again, as if his presence did not bother her.

"I gave you the blue necklace so you would arrange for me to trade my goods with your people," Lewis Casler said.

"You did not give me the necklace. You threw it away, and I found it," Dawn Light said. She spoke boldly, but she was still trembling inside.

"Why aren't you wearing it now?" Lewis Casler said with an evil smile.

"Because I threw it away," Dawn Light lied.

"You foolish girl!" Lewis Casler growled. "You have brought bad luck to your clan!"

"That's not so," Dawn Light said. "The necklace was not made by the Creator, so it has no spirit."

Casler laughed a cruel laugh. "Tell that to my grandmother," he said. "She wore that necklace for years after my grandfather gave it to her. Day and night, she was never without it. One day she took it off, saying she was tired of it. By the end of the day, she was dead!"

Still laughing, he turned and disappeared into the forest.

When he had gone, Dawn Light leaned on her hoe and took several deep breaths to calm herself. It can't be, she told herself. The necklace cannot have an evil spirit. Casler is just trying to scare me.

Suddenly Gray Shell came running up. "Dawn Light!" she said. "Lewis Casler was in the village just now!"

"I know," Dawn Light answered. "He was just here."

"With you?" Gray Shell asked in surprise. "What did he want?"

"He was angry because we will not trade with him. I told him I had thrown away the blue necklace, and that made him even angrier," Dawn Light said.

"Good!" Gray Shell said. "Now maybe he will not come here again."

Dawn Light did not tell her friend that she hadn't thrown away the necklace. She knew Gray Shell would insist that she do so. But she couldn't, remembering how it had shone in the sunlight. Besides, no bad luck had come to the clan yet, other than the whitefaces moving closer. But they had been doing that long before she had found the necklace. Casler had lied to her, she was sure. For now, the beautiful blue beads would stay where they were.

"When will you wear the silver necklace Jeremy Cairns gave you?" Gray Shell asked. "It is so pretty!"

Dawn Light reached into her dress then and pulled out the necklace. "I wear it all the time," she said.

"But why don't you wear it so that all can see?" Gray Shell taunted. "Could it be that you are afraid to do so?"

Dawn Light frowned. "Afraid? Why should I be afraid?" she asked.

"Because Falling Water might be hurt to see that you accepted such a fine gift from another young man," Gray Shell said.

Dawn Light flushed angrily. "Don't be silly, cousin!" she said.

But she admitted to herself that the thought *had* crossed her mind. Wearing the silver necklace given to her by the white boy might hurt Falling Water's feelings. And so she kept it hidden under her dress. For the first time, Dawn Light realized that she actually cared about Falling Water's feelings.

* * *

That afternoon two white men came to the village. Dawn Light recognized them as two of the family who lived in the new cabin. They had angry looks on their faces.

Loud Thunder went to talk to the men while others in the village watched warily.

"Welcome," Loud Thunder said. "What brings you to visit us?"

"We've got a pretty good idea your people here have been stealing our chickens," said the older man, whose name was Albert Wyatt.

His son looked around and spotted Black Wing standing nearby with Falling Water. The white boy sneered at Black Wing, as if mocking him about the deer incident.

"Our people are not thieves," Loud Thunder assured them in a calm voice.

Albert Wyatt glanced over at where Dawn Light and Gray Shell stood. "Those two," he said, pointing at the girls. "We caught them spying on us. We think they were scouting for their menfolk. That's when they saw how easy it'd be to break into our chicken coop."

"Why do you blame the Iroquois when there are many strangers in the wilderness?" Loud Thunder asked.

"The fence around our chicken coop was cut and ten chickens were taken," the white man said. "We've got no other neighbors except the Cairnses. And they sure wouldn't do it. Seems to me that the only ones who'd do a low-down stunt like chicken stealing would be you Iroquois."

Dawn Light glanced at her grandmother as the white man spoke. Although the old woman's face showed no emotion, her eyes were suddenly filled with anger. And Dawn Light knew why. Cloud Shadow now knew the truth about how her grandson and his friend had come by the chickens. And she also knew that they had blatantly lied to her.

"We are not thieves," Loud Thunder reiterated, keeping his voice even.

"Well, we're giving you fair notice," Wyatt warned. "Me and my boys are armed. And if we see any of your people anywhere near our cabin, we're going to kill them on the spot. Just like we'd kill a weasel poaching our birds. Just watch yourselves, because we'll *not* be robbed."

With that the man and his son turned and left the village.

Dawn Light glanced around for Black Wing and Falling Water. But it was as if they had vanished.

Then she looked at her grandmother. Cloud Shadow looked grim. She, too, was scanning the area for the two boys. Dawn Light trembled for her brother and Falling Water when the old grandmother finally found them.

7 Dawn Light searched the entire village for Black Wing and Falling Water but could not find them. She assumed that they had taken to the woods.

When she returned home, she saw that a deep sense of gloom had settled over the longhouse. Her relatives were disappointed in Black Wing for the lie he had told. And they were frightened of what the Wyatts might do if they discovered the truth.

Since the truth was out now, Dawn Light decided to tell her grandmother the entire story.

"Not long ago, Black Wing was tracking a deer," the girl began. "Albert Wyatt's sons menaced Black Wing and shot the deer for themselves. Black Wing went to their cabin with the intention of fighting the oldest Wyatt boy. But Falling Water convinced him to steal their chickens instead."

"Falling Water is gaining wisdom," Cloud Shadow observed. "Stealing chickens is better than fighting. But we must still find the boys and bring them home. What they did may have been just in their eyes, but the white man does not accept such justice. If Albert Wyatt finds them in the woods alone, away from the village, he may do violence to them."

"I know of places in the forest where my brother goes," Dawn Light said. "But if they see men from the village looking for them, they will run and hide in another place. Please allow Gray Shell and me to search for them. If they see us, they will show themselves. Then we can tell them it's safe to come home."

Cloud Shadow nodded solemnly. "Go then, and find them," she said.

Dawn Light and Gray Shell set out into the forest in search of the boys. They hurried so that they might find them before dark.

"Black Wing likes to go to where the red raspberry grows," Dawn Light said. "It is a slope where the brush is very thick, not far from the stream. Follow me."

Dawn Light led the way, and they soon arrived at the spot she had described.

Both girls looked around but saw no sign of the two boys. Dawn Light cupped her hands around her mouth. She was about to call out Black Wing's name when a different sound met her ear. Gray Shell heard it too. The girls froze and stared at each other. It was the sound of an ax biting wood, and it was very close.

"Shhhh!" Dawn Light said, grasping Gray Shell's arm tightly and pulling her cousin down into the brush. The girls peered out to see a white man swinging an ax at a huge pine tree. He was not a hundred yards away from them.

Again and again the man struck at the tree until at last the ancient pine fell. It made Dawn Light heartsick to see the stately tree crash to the forest floor.

Suddenly another white-faced man appeared and began swinging at the trunk of another white pine nearer the stream.

"They are clearing the land for more cabins!" Gray Shell whispered to Dawn Light.

Dawn Light suddenly felt a great sense of foreboding descend upon her. This was the closest yet that the whitefaces had come to the Iroquois village! Here was where Dawn Light and her brother collected leaves for tea and where they gathered raspberries by the basketful. Here was where Dawn Light's mother and grandmother had played as little girls. Soon all the trees here would be cut down, and more cabins would rise— fenced-in places where Iroquois were forbidden to go.

Stealthily, Dawn Light and Gray Shell hurried off in another direction to look for the two boys. Had Black Wing seen the new clearing too? How angry it would have made him! Maybe angry enough to do something desperate. And this time perhaps Falling Water would not be able to stop him.

Dawn Light searched all the places she knew her brother liked to go. But there was no sign of either Falling Water or Black Wing. Finally, in the dusk, the girls wearily began their journey home, taking a different way this time in the hopes of finding the boys.

Not far from the village, Gray Shell suddenly laid her hand on Dawn Light's arm. "Cousin," she said with dread in her voice, "look!"

A little ways off the path lay Black Wing, face down on the forest floor.

"Hurry! Run to the village for help!" Dawn Light cried. She stayed by her brother as Gray Shell hurried off.

Dawn Light turned her brother over and saw with horror that he had been shot in the chest. Underneath his still body lay a musket, the barrel of which had exploded. It had obviously backfired when Black Wing had tried to defend himself against whoever shot him. Dawn Light recognized it as one of the muskets from the Casler brothers.

"Oh, Black Wing!" Dawn Light wailed. "Why did you leave the village today? Why didn't you stay and take your punishment for stealing the white man's birds? Surely you'd be alive now."

A few minutes later, Loud Thunder and several other men hurried to where Dawn Light waited. Sadly Loud Thunder lifted the body of his son off the ground and set off toward the village. Out of respect, the others followed several paces behind.

As the village began the mourning ritual for Black Wing, Cloud Shadow sent a runner to Mort Cairns' cabin to ask Cairns to come at once. He was the only white man the Iroquois knew who might see that justice was done.

At dawn the next morning, Mort Cairns arrived and was taken immediately to Cloud Shadow.

"The son of my daughter has been murdered by a white man," Cloud Shadow began. "We found him in the forest where the Iroquois have every right to be."

"I am truly sorry to hear that, Cloud Shadow," Mort Cairns replied. "His family is indeed a fine family, and this is a great loss to them."

"Black Wing's blood cries out for justice," Cloud Shadow continued. "Can you help us obtain it for him?"

"There is very little I can do," Mort Cairns admitted. "We don't even know who killed your grandson."

"There are treaties between the Iroquois and the United States government," Cloud Shadow reminded the man. "Do they not say that we can live here in peace and not be murdered in the forest at will?"

"The white man will probably claim that

he was defending himself," Mort Cairns explained. "Remember, Black Wing had a musket too. No white man's court would blame a settler for protecting himself against an Indian with a gun."

"So," Cloud Thunder said bitterly, "the whitefaces come to kill the forest. One by one the trees fall. And now they come to kill us."

Sadly Mort Cairns said, "I am one of those white men who have come to your forest. I mean you no harm. And I would like nothing better than for the Iroquois to continue living the way they have always lived. But that is not the way all white people feel. And in my heart I have always known that this would happen sooner or later. By being on good terms with you, I have simply attempted to put it off as long as possible."

"The Iroquois thank you for the friendship you have shown us in the past," the wise old woman said. "But now our friendship must end. The Iroquois can no longer afford to trust any whitefaces. Please go away and do not return to our village."

"But our trading—" the white man began.

"We will trade no more—with you or any whiteface," Cloud Shadow declared. "My daughter Deer Path was right. We need nothing from the whitefaces."

She turned away from the man to show that the meeting had ended.

Mort Cairns sighed then and nodded in understanding. Then he left the village.

All day long, Dawn Light sat with her relatives by the body of Black Wing. Only yesterday, his dark, piercing eyes had dominated his handsome face. But now his eyes were closed forever. His long, raven-colored hair framed his still features, but the windows of his soul were dark.

Dawn Light thought back to the merry days of their childhood. She could still hear the laughter they had shared. It floated to her as if from a dream. But Black Wing would not laugh on this earth again. And his strong voice would no longer ring through the forest. Her brother had gone to the world of the spirits. There would be days of singing mournful songs in the village, Dawn Light knew. And then the body of Black Wing would be buried.

"Brother," Dawn Light whispered, "I am sorry I could not find you in time to bring you home safely. And I am sorry for the times I grieved you. But I will never forget the things you taught me. You go now to the heavenly fields where the sun never tires of shining, and the rivers sparkle, and the forests will stand forever."

Suddenly Dawn Light was gripped by an almost overwhelming bitterness toward the whitefaces. Why are we not able to live with our forest untouched and our people safe? she wondered. Though it saddened her, she understood that the Iroquois who had sided with the British in the great war had been punished by being driven from their lands. But it had never been so for her people. Why did the treaty her people had made with the white man's government mean nothing?

Suddenly her hand went to the silver necklace hidden under her dress, and she thought of Jeremy Cairns. Light-haired, blue-eyed Jeremy, who had given her the beautiful gift. And Meg and Josh, who were always delighted to see her. How could she deny their friendship? she asked herself. But then Dawn Light shook her head resolutely. She knew that she could never feel the same toward the Cairns children—or any other white people—again.

* * *

Falling Water had not been seen in the village since the day Black Wing died. The men had searched the forest for him, afraid of discovering his body as well. But they had found nothing.

Dawn Light was troubled by the disappearance of her brother's friend. And she couldn't help wondering if Lewis Casler had been right after all. Were the blue beads possessed by an evil spirit after all? And had that spirit caused the trouble that had struck her village—the death of Black Wing and the disappearance of Falling Water?

One evening when the village had quieted down for the night, Dawn Light sneaked away to the oddly shaped tree where she had buried the blue necklace. She dug until she uncovered the deerskin pouch. Then she removed the necklace and held it up in the moonlight. Instead of shining gaily, the beads now gleamed with an eerie glow. How could I have ever thought these beads beautiful? she wondered. Her heart was filled with hatred as she gazed at them. She stood up then, held the necklace high over her head, and hurled it into the stream. Then she did the same with the silver necklace from Jeremy Cairns.

She wanted nothing from the white-faced people, the murderers of the forest and the murderers of her brother. "I will take nothing again and give nothing again," she vowed aloud.

Then she turned to go—and was suddenly face-to-face with Falling Water.

"Do not make a sound," he cautioned, but Dawn Light couldn't help gasping. It seemed that Falling Water had aged into an old man since the day he had run away. He had lost weight, and his face was deeply lined. Even his strong, straight shoulders were now sloped, as if they carried an onerous burden. He led her into the trees where they could speak without being seen.

"Black Wing is dead," Dawn Light whispered.

"I know," Falling Water said. "And I will soon avenge him."

"Were you with him when he died?" Dawn Light asked.

"No," Falling Water said. "We went into the forest together to hunt. We took two muskets with us, hoping to get a deer. We hunted all day but could find no deer—or any game worth taking, thanks to the white settlers! But we did spy Lewis Casler and his brother headed toward the village. We knew they would try to trade their worthless wares for our beaver pelts again. Black Wing wanted to confront them, to tell them to stay away from the village. But I talked him out of it. A little while later, we stopped to rest. I fell asleep, and I thought Black Wing slept as well. But when I awoke, he was gone. I called for him, but he didn't answer. So I went looking for him. That is when I came upon his body."

"What do you think happened?" Dawn Light asked.

"I think he crossed paths with the Casler brothers," Falling Water replied. "Black Wing had a hot temper, and they probably knew that his musket would not work. And so they killed him. But I will avenge my friend and brother. I will kill the Casler brothers. *And* I will drive back the white cabin builders—in Black Wing's name!"

"You will die in such a cause," Dawn Light said quietly.

"I will become as a shadow in the forest," Falling Water said. "They will not know where I am before I put an end to them. Word will spread that a bad spirit inhabits the trees. And the rest of the cabin builders will leave the forest to the Iroquois."

Dawn Light admired Falling Water for his devotion to her brother. But she knew his mission was doomed. If he killed Lewis Casler, or any other white man, the rage of the white-faced people would descend upon the whole tribe. Armed men would come and surround them as they had surrounded the Conestoga people, killing men, women, and children alike. Or maybe soldiers would come and drive her people away, as they had done to the Iroquois who had sided with the British.

"You cannot win, Falling Water," Dawn Light said sadly.

"But I can fight," Falling Water said. "I can fight as long as I am alive!"

"I must go now," Falling Water said.

"No. Come back to the village," Dawn Light pleaded, tears forming in her eyes. "It is safe there."

Falling Water shook his head and smiled a sad smile. "I can't," he said. "I must try to help my people. And I can't do that by sitting idly in the village, waiting for the white people to push us off our land." He laid a hand on Dawn Light's arm then. "Before I go, you must make a promise, Dawn Light. Promise not to tell anyone that you have seen me."

"But—" the girl began.

Falling Water placed a finger on Dawn Light's lips. "If our people know I am still in the forest, they will come after me and force me to go back. Let them think I have run away—or that I am dead. Only then can I do what needs to be done."

A tear slipped down Dawn Light's cheek, and Falling Water gently wiped it away. "Promise?" he asked.

"I promise," Dawn Light whispered.

Falling Water lifted Dawn Light's face up and placed a soft kiss upon her lips. As he did so, Dawn Light closed her eyes. "Take care, Dawn Light," she heard Falling Water say.

When she opened her eyes, Falling Water was gone. He had disappeared so quickly that she wondered if, indeed, he was a spirit of the forest.

As she turned to make her way back to the village, Dawn Light thought about the young man she had once thought she was destined to marry. She knew there was little chance of that now. He would fight his doomed crusade to avenge the death of Black Wing, and he would die. And the thought of his death made Dawn Light's heart ache greatly.

How many times had she plotted to avoid marrying him? she wondered. And now, when at last she admired him and felt affection toward him, she would lose him. Now when she could accept and even embrace the idea of marrying Falling Water, it would not come to pass. It seemed to her the cruelest turn of fate of all.

8 The next day, He-Who-Dreams gathered the elders of the village for a meeting. They discussed the increased number of white settlers in the forest.

"They will push us off our land, as they have so many before us," one of the men said.

"But there is a treaty that says we can live here forever," another pointed out.

"The treaty does not mean anything," the first man countered. "The army of the United States will not come to save our forest."

Derisive laughter spread through the frightened, angry group. Everyone knew the army would never turn back the white cabin builders.

He-Who-Dreams stood up then and called for silence. "Before, I thought we could live in peace with the whitefaces," he began. "Now I realize I was wrong. We must not stay here any longer. We must leave before we are starved out, or forced out, or murdered."

"But where will we go?" an old woman cried.

"To Canada where the Iroquois before us have gone," the *sachem* replied. "The treaties the Canadians make with the Iroquois are not broken. We will find a place where we can live in peace and where our children can prosper."

He called for a vote then. When the elders had finished voting, it was decided that the turtle clan would move north after the winter.

The thought of leaving the only home she had ever known filled Dawn Light with sadness. Even worse was the fear that Falling Water would still be a renegade in the forest when they left. And Dawn Light would never see him again. She would never even know his fate.

A few days later, one of the young boys of the village discovered a badly wounded white man lying near the edge of the forest. It looked as if the man had been heading toward the village when he collapsed. Several men brought the unconscious man into the village.

"It is Mort Cairns," Cloud Shadow said.

Dawn Light felt horror course through her body. Had Falling Water shot Mort

Cairns? she worried. Falling Water had sworn vengeance on all the white cabin builders!

She looked at Cloud Shadow then, wondering what the old woman would do. She had sent Mort Cairns away after Black Wing had been killed. Would she help him now? Dawn Light wondered.

"Take him into the longhouse," Cloud Shadow ordered. "And summon the shaman."

Loud Thunder and another man carried Mort Cairns into the longhouse of Dawn Light's family. There they laid him on a platform. A musket ball had torn off his right ear and left a terrible gash in his head, but he was still alive.

Cloud Shadow finished cleansing the wound just as the shaman arrived. Soon after, the longhouse was filled with steam from medicinal roots and the chanting of the medicine man.

"Who could have done this horrible deed?" Cloud Shadow worried as she sat next to her granddaughter. "If the shaman's efforts fail, and Mort Cairns dies here, the whitefaces will blame his death on us."

Dawn Light knew then that she should tell Cloud Shadow about Falling Water's vow. She had promised Falling Water she would tell no one, it was true. But the safety of the village was at stake now. And her grandmother deserved to know everything so that she could make a decision about what to do.

"Grandmother," Dawn Light began. "I spoke to Falling Water in the forest a few days ago. He is very angry that Black Wing died and has set out to avenge my brother's death."

Cloud Shadow looked shocked. "And how will he do this?" she asked, dread creeping into her voice.

"He vowed to kill all the cabin builders in the forest," Dawn Light said. "In this way, he hopes to drive the whitefaces away."

Cloud Shadow thought a long moment before speaking again. "We must let no one know that Mort Cairns is here," she finally told Dawn Light. "We must hide him. If the shaman's medicine works, then we will ask the red-beard who shot him. If he says it was Falling Water, then we must keep the white man prisoner until we are safe in Canada. Then we will let him go."

"And what if Mort Cairns dies here, Grandmother?" Dawn Light asked.

"Then we will hide his body far from here—where no one will ever find it," Cloud Shadow replied.

Dawn Light sighed. Neither course of action was easy. She thought about the Cairns family then. She knew they must be very worried just as her family had been worried when Black Wing didn't come home. But there was no help for that. Cloud Shadow was right. If the white people knew the badly wounded man was in the village, they would surmise the Iroquois had shot him. And the disaster Lewis Casler had predicted for her people would be complete.

9 The next morning, Dawn Light met Jeremy Cairns heading toward the village. His blue eyes were filled with worry, and Dawn Light's heart went out to him, in spite of herself. She took him to see Cloud Shadow.

"My father went into the forest early yesterday morning," Jeremy explained. "And he was bound for here. He has not returned, and we are all worried."

Cloud Shadow stood at the door of her longhouse, her arms folded. "If we see him, we will tell him that his family is looking for him," she said in a stoic voice.

Inside the longhouse, Mort Cairns still lay unconscious. Deer Path stood nearby to stifle any cry he might make in his delirium while Jeremy was near.

"He might have met friends and gone off in another direction," Jeremy said, "but I can't escape the feeling that he is in trouble."

"Perhaps he was tracking a deer, and it took him far from his home," Cloud Shadow said, still not moving from the doorway. "We will send a runner to your cabin if your father comes here."

"Thank you," Jeremy replied. Then he turned and went on his way.

"It hurts me that we could not tell him his father is here," Dawn Light said.

"Don't be foolish, child," Cloud Shadow warned. "To be ruled by feelings is foolish. Remember the Conestoga people. One member of the tribe was suspected of a crime, and all were destroyed."

Dawn Light knew her grandmother was right. But she couldn't help feeling sorry for Jeremy. Out of habit, her hand went to her neck. And she couldn't help feeling a pang of longing for the silver necklace that was no longer there.

* * *

In the early evening, Dawn Light went to the stream to get a bucket of water for the longhouse. As she dipped her bucket into the rushing water, she heard the sad cry of a dove nearby. She looked around to catch a glimpse of the bird but saw nothing.

Suddenly Dawn Light smiled. There was only one person she knew of who could so accurately mimic a dove.

"Falling Water!" Dawn Light cried as the young man emerged from the forest.

Falling Water came closer. He looked even leaner than before. His hair was longer, and it lay in tangles on his shoulders.

"Does the red-bearded man still live?" Falling Water asked.

Falling Water's question was like a knife to Dawn Light's heart. So he knew Mort Cairns had been shot!

"Y-yes," Dawn Light stammered. "But the shaman is still with him."

Falling Water nodded but said nothing.

"Oh, Falling Water," Dawn Light cried, "are you the one who did him harm?"

"No," Falling Water replied. "But I was afraid you would think that. And that is why I waited for you here tonight."

"But . . . you vowed to avenge Black Wing's death," Dawn Light said. "You said you would hide in the forest and—"

"Yes, but I would never hurt the red-beard," Falling Water interrupted. "He has never meant us any harm. I only hoped to scare him away. But yesterday I found him gravely wounded in the forest. I carried him to the edge of the village so that someone might find him and help him."

Dawn Light stared at Falling Water in relief. "Forgive me for my evil thoughts," she said. "It broke my heart to think that you were guilty of such a thing."

"I am glad that your heart is not broken," Falling Water smiled. "Now I must go. It is dangerous for me to be seen."

Dawn Light looked with sadness at the young man before her. She wanted desperately to plead with him again to stay. But she knew that to do so would be futile. Falling Water was on a mission, and he would not give it up. No matter what happened.

So instead of allowing the tears to come, she took a deep breath and said, "Good-bye, Falling Water. Please be careful."

And again he was gone in the blink of an eye.

Dawn Light returned to the longhouse then and sat beside Mort Cairns. He was still unconscious, but his chest heaved up and down with life. And that filled Dawn

Light with hope. Perhaps he will live after all, she thought.

The shaman had certainly done all he could. He had crooned and chanted and used his most powerful medicine: healing herbs, four snakeskins, a woodpecker's head, and a squirrel skin. Now it was simply a matter of waiting.

* * *

The next morning, Dawn Light heard voices of white men outside the longhouse. She felt a rush of terror. Had they found out that Mort Cairns was in the village?

Hurriedly she dressed and ran outside. She was relieved to see that it was only the Casler brothers with some old kettles and whiskey to trade. She hung back so that Lewis Casler would not see her.

Robert Casler rubbed his chin with the back of his dirty hand and said, "We've come to trade for beaver pelts."

"We don't want to trade with you," Loud Thunder said.

Lewis Casler laughed. "Well, if you're thinking of trading with Mort Cairns, you can give up that notion," he said. "He's dead."

Dawn Light caught her breath. How did Casler know of the shooting? If he did not commit the crime, how did he know? Suddenly Dawn Light came to a new conclusion. The Caslers didn't know that Cloud Shadow had sent Mort Cairns away. They thought the Iroquois were still trading with him. And the only way to steal his trade with the Iroquois was to kill him!

"How did the man die?" asked Cloud Shadow, coming out of the longhouse.

Lewis Casler laughed again and said, "He was shot dead, that's what he was. Shot through the head—probably by some skulking Indian."

"Yeah," Robert said. "I hear tell some young brave has been attacking white people in the forest. It was probably him."

Dawn Light stole a glance at her grandmother to see if Cloud Shadow would react to what Robert Casler said. But the old woman's face registered no emotion.

"You think such a thing to be true, and

yet you come to trade with Iroquois murderers?" Cloud Shadow pointed out.

Both men shrugged. "We're not afraid of anybody—red or white," Lewis Casler said. "Anyway, I never liked Cairns. He's been stealing our trade for a long time. I'm glad he's out of the way. More trade for my brother and me."

"Where is the body of the red-beard?" Cloud Shadow asked slyly. "How can we believe he's dead if we don't see his body? Maybe he is on a hunting trip and will soon return. Then he will expect our beaver pelts in trade. If we trade our pelts with you, what will we have for our friend and brother if he returns?"

Lewis Casler sneered and said, "He ain't coming back. You can count on that. But we can show you the body if you want. It's probably still lying in the forest. That is, if the wild things haven't carried it away. "

"Loud Thunder, go with the brothers to see Mort Cairns' body," Cloud Shadow said. Then she turned back to the white men. "If what you say is true, we will trade with you from now on," she said.

"Oh, it's true, all right," Lewis Casler

said, smiling smugly. The two set off into the forest with Loud Thunder.

When they were gone, Dawn Light went to look for Gray Shell. She found her weaving a rug.

"Cousin," Dawn Light said, "come quickly!"

"Why?" Gray Shell wanted to know.

"Don't ask questions. Just come," Dawn Light replied. "I'll tell you on the way."

Gray Shell put her weaving away and joined her cousin. As the girls headed into the forest, Dawn Light explained about the Caslers taking Loud Thunder to see Mort Cairns' body.

"I want to see what happens when they can't find the red-beard," Dawn Light said. "But be very quiet. I don't want them to know we are near."

They followed the voices of the Casler brothers they could hear in front of them.

"You won't be sorry if you trade with us, Loud Thunder," Robert Casler was saying. "We have come upon many fine, new things your people can use."

"He's right here," Robert Casler said a few minutes later.

Silently the girls moved closer until they had a good view of the three men.

"We found him shot through the head by this tree," his brother added.

"I don't see him," Loud Thunder said, looking around.

Lewis Casler looked agitated. "I know this is the tree, isn't it, Robert? Maybe he wasn't quite dead, and he crawled off to die. Let's have a look around."

For some time, the Caslers searched the surrounding brush, their frustration growing with every minute.

Finally Loud Thunder announced, "Mort Cairns is not here. Not until you can show us his body will we trade with you."

He headed back toward the village then.

"Listen up!" Lewis Casler called to Loud Thunder. "We'll find that body, and then we'll be back to the village to trade for beaver pelts!"

Dawn Light watched her father leave. Then she glanced back and saw the Casler brothers, eyes to the ground. They were moving farther away now, still searching for Mort Cairns' body.

Dawn Light laid a hand on Gray Shell's arm and whispered. "Gray Shell, let's stay close to them," she said. "Maybe we will hear them say something about shooting Mort Cairns."

"But they will speak English," Gray Shell pointed out.

"I now understand a few words," Dawn Light said. "Meg Cairns taught me. And I've listened closely to my father's translations. I think I could make out some of what they say."

"All right," Gray Shell said.

The two girls moved closer to where the two men were. They crouched down, shrouded by the brush.

"I don't understand," Lewis Casler said. "He was right here."

"You sure you killed him?" Robert muttered. "You never could shoot worth a darn. Maybe he got up and ran home!"

"Shut up, you fool," Lewis Casler seethed. "I killed Mort Cairns. I shot him with my gun—through the head. Believe me, he was dead. He had to be."

Dawn Light understood enough of Lewis Casler's words to realize that he had just confessed to shooting Mort Cairns. She signaled to Gray Shell that they could leave. Silently, the two girls moved off.

"He admitted it!" Dawn Light said to her cousin as they headed down the path. "Lewis Casler just said that he shot the red-beard."

"Let's get back to Cloud Shadow and tell her what we heard," Gray Shell said.

The girls hurried into the village and to the longhouse of Dawn Light's family. They told Cloud Shadow what they had heard.

"So now we know the names of the murderers," Cloud Shadow said. "But if Mort Cairns does not live, we will have no way to convince the white people of the truth. They stick with their own, even if it be with evil men like the Caslers. The words of one bad white man are worth more than the words of an entire Iroquois village."

Two days later, Mort Cairns opened his eyes. His hand went immediately to his wound. "What happened?" he rasped.

Dawn Light brought him a drink of

water as Loud Thunder explained about finding him injured near the forest.

Cloud Shadow nodded. "You have been asleep for many days," she said.

"Thank you for taking care of me," Cairns said.

"Do you remember who did this to you?" Cloud Shadow asked.

Mort Cairns looked blank. Then suddenly he said, "It was the Casler brothers! I don't know which one shot me, but I ran into them in the forest. They told me they were tired of losing trade to me and were going to stop me once and for all. That's all I remember."

He was quiet for a moment. Suddenly he frowned. "No, wait!" he said. "I do recall something more. I remember someone picking me up and carrying me for what seemed like a long ways. He laid me down then and disappeared."

"That was Falling Water, Grandmother," Dawn Light said.

"Well, I'm much obliged to him," Mort Cairns said. "If it weren't for him—and for you people—I wouldn't be alive."

Cloud Shadow nodded, obviously

pleased. "Go now, child," she said. "Run to the red-beard's cabin and tell his family that he is alive."

Dawn Light ran swiftly and happily. She was glad Mort Cairns would live. And she was glad her people would not be blamed for it. Perhaps, she thought, things would be different now. Maybe Mort Cairns would tell the whitefaces how the people of the turtle clan had cared for him. Maybe then the whitefaces would honor the treaty the government had with the Iroquois. And then maybe they would not have to abandon their beloved village and move to Canada.

When she reached the small cabin, Dawn Light pounded on the door. Mort Cairns' wife came to the door, wiping her hands on her apron. She looked quizzically at Dawn Light.

"Mort Cairns—alive! Come!" Dawn Light said in English.

"What?" the woman asked in amazement.

"Lewis Casler shoot Mort Cairns," Dawn Light said. "Iroquois help him. Come!"

"Praise be to God!" the yellow-braided woman cried.

By now the children had appeared. "It's Pa! He's alive!" Josh yelled.

"Boys! Go with her!" Mrs. Cairns said joyfully. "Bring your father home!"

Jeremy saddled the horse and then led it back through the forest with Dawn Light and Josh. Once they reached the village, the two boys ran into the longhouse to see for themselves that their father was alive. Many of the villagers were on hand to see the happy reunion.

"I'm uglier than I was, but I'm alive!" Mort Cairns said, embracing both sons in his huge arms. He looked at the russet-colored faces gathered around him. "I owe you a lot, my friends," he said, wiping away a tear of joy. "And I aim to repay you."

Loud Thunder and another man helped Mort Cairns onto the horse then, and his sons took him home.

10 Summer came to an end, and still Falling Water did not return to his people. Almost every night, Dawn Light waited by the stream for his dove cry, but she waited in vain. Dawn Light assumed that Falling Water had left the area since they had heard no more reports of attacks on white settlers. She grieved for his loss and went to sleep each night on her beaver robe hoping he would return.

That fall, a sadness permeated the regular routines of the village. Every crop that was harvested brought with it the knowledge that there would be no more crops from this earth. Every glossy beaver pelt was a reminder that no more pelts would come to them from Brother Beaver. And every leaf that turned to brilliant orange or sunflower gold told them that soon they would leave their beloved forest.

Still, Dawn Light clung to the hope that maybe they wouldn't have to go to Canada. One day she asked her grandmother about it.

"Come, child," Cloud Shadow replied.

Dawn Light followed her grandmother out of the village and into the bluffs that rose above a nearby river. When they reached the top of the highest hill, they stopped. From their vantage point, they could see the forest that spread to the south and west. Dawn Light had never seen the forest from above before and was struck by the vastness of it.

Cloud Shadow silently pointed off into the distance. In the midst of all the trees, Dawn Light could see at least ten new clearings. The sounds of axes crashed in the chilly air as the cabin builders hurried to finish their homes before winter.

"In the spring, there will be even more white settlers and fewer trees," Cloud Shadow said grimly.

It was then that Dawn Light knew that the forest was doomed and there was no turning back. That no matter what Falling Water had done or was doing to stop the cabin builders, they would not be evicted from the land they now claimed as rightfully theirs.

"Do you understand now why we must go?" Cloud Shadow asked gently.

Dawn Light nodded, tears brimming in her eyes. "Yes, Grandmother," she whispered. "We must go."

In the early spring, the turtle clan began their hectic preparations for the trek north. They emptied the bark-lined storage pits of corn. They would carry the corn with them and dig new storage pits in Canada. Iroquois hunters ranged far and wide now, taking deer and curing the meat into jerky. They filled baskets with dried berries to eat and seeds for their next harvest. They packed their pots and utensils, and the wampum belts, woven with designs that told the history of the clan.

Finally everything was ready to go. The villagers would sleep one last night in their longhouses and then set out in the morning.

With a deep melancholy, Dawn Light wandered the village, taking a last, longing look at the only place she had known as home. Here was the longhouse of White Eagle, whose men were the best archers in the village. There was the longhouse of her grandmother's friend,

Laughing Brook, whose women made the most beautiful baskets. And here was the longhouse of Falling Water's relatives. Dawn Light wondered how they felt, leaving their young warrior behind with no way to tell him where they were going. And at the thought of Falling Water, the sadness within Dawn Light deepened. She missed the young man desperately, more than she ever thought she would.

When she returned to her longhouse, she saw that Mort Cairns and his family had come to say good-bye. All three children were there. And even the mother with the thick, yellow braids had come.

"I told you I'd repay you for your kindness," Mort Cairns was telling Loud Thunder.

The red-beard took down several packs from his horse, and Josh and Jeremy began opening them and laying the contents on the ground for all to see. By now, many of the villagers had gathered.

In the first pack were fine knives of various sizes. In the next pack, were several bolts of brightly colored cloth.

And still another pack held copper and iron kettles, the kind that wouldn't crack.

The villagers smiled and nodded in approval. Dawn Light hung back though, not willing to be lifted from her somber mood. But when all the wares had been displayed, Jeremy sought her out.

"Hello, Dawn Light," he said.

Dawn Light managed a smile and nodded.

"I am sorry you have to go," the boy continued in broken Iroquois.

When Dawn Light did not respond, he said, "Before you go, I wanted you to know that my father went to the authorities and told them what Lewis Casler did. They arrested him, and he's now being held in jail, awaiting trial."

"Thank you," Dawn Light said. "That is good to know." But she couldn't help wondering if justice would be done for the death of Black Wing. More than likely, she thought, Lewis Casler will be set free.

"Oh, and I brought you something" Jeremy added. He reached into his pocket and took out a silver necklace. It was even more resplendent than the first one he had given her. From the necklace dangled a pearly pendant that reflected the sun's light.

"It's an abalone shell," Jeremy said. "From the ocean." He handed the necklace to Dawn Light. "Put it on," he said.

Dawn Light hesitated. She had sworn to herself that she would never take a gift from a whiteface again.

"Please," Jeremy said. "It's a gift of friendship. I want us to be friends— forever."

Dawn Light looked into Jeremy's bright blue eyes and saw the good soul that existed there. The same good soul that existed in Josh and Meg, and Mort Cairns and his wife. And she knew then that she could never hate Jeremy or his family. She knew that her father was right. Just as there were good Iroquois and bad Iroquois, so were there both good and bad whitefaces. And this light-haired boy with eyes the color of the sky would always be her friend, no matter how many miles separated them.

Dawn Light fastened the necklace

around her neck. Jeremy smiled in approval.

Dawn Light smiled back. "Pretty maiden?" she asked in English.

Jeremy nodded. "Pretty maiden," he replied.

* * *

The next day the 300 Iroquois headed north, each carrying a piece of the village they had left behind. The long column of people hurried. They knew they must reach their new home soon. In early spring the bark they needed to build new longhouses was easiest to peel from the elm trees. And they had to prepare the new earth to receive their precious seeds for the fall harvest.

Tears streamed down Dawn Light's face as she walked along, carrying a basketful of corn. But she did not look back. She let the wind dry the tears as she headed for her new home. She had to be strong, like her mother and grandmother and great-grandmother before her.

As she walked, she thought of Falling

Water and wondered where he was. Perhaps he was dead, she thought sadly. Perhaps an angry white-face had shot him. If so, she would never know. But dead or alive, Dawn Light silently wished him well.

Suddenly someone tall and strong reached out and grasped her hand. Dawn Light turned her head, expecting to see that her father had come to comfort her. Instead, she found herself looking into the dark eyes of Falling Water. He smiled, and with his free hand, took the basket from her. With their chins held high and their shoulders thrown back, they walked north with their people.

* * *

The turtle clan built a new village near Brantford, Ontario, in Canada. The following spring, Dawn Light and Falling Water laid their firstborn son in a cradle board decorated with symbols from the turtle clan. Their descendants still live in Canada today.

Novels by Anne Schraff

PASSAGES

An Alien Spring
Bridge to the Moon (Sequel to *Maitland's Kid*)
The Darkest Secret
Don't Blame the Children
The Ghost Boy
The Haunting of Hawthorne
Maitland's Kid
Please Don't Ask Me to Love You
The Power of the Rose (Sequel to *The Haunting of Hawthorne*)
The Shadow Man
The Shining Mark (Sequel to *When a Hero Dies*)
A Song to Sing
Sparrow's Treasure
Summer of Shame (Sequel to *An Alien Spring*)
To Slay the Dragon (Sequel to *Don't Blame the Children*)
The Vandal
When a Hero Dies

PASSAGES 2000

The Boy from Planet Nowhere
Gingerbread Heart
The Hyena Laughs at Night
Just Another Name for Lonely (Sequel to *Please Don't Ask Me to Love You*)
Memories Are Forever

PASSAGES to History

And We Will Be No More
The Bloody Wake of the *Infamy*
Dear Mr. Kilmer
Dream Mountain
Hear That Whistle Blow
Strawberry Autumn
Winter at Wolf Crossing
The Witches of Northboro